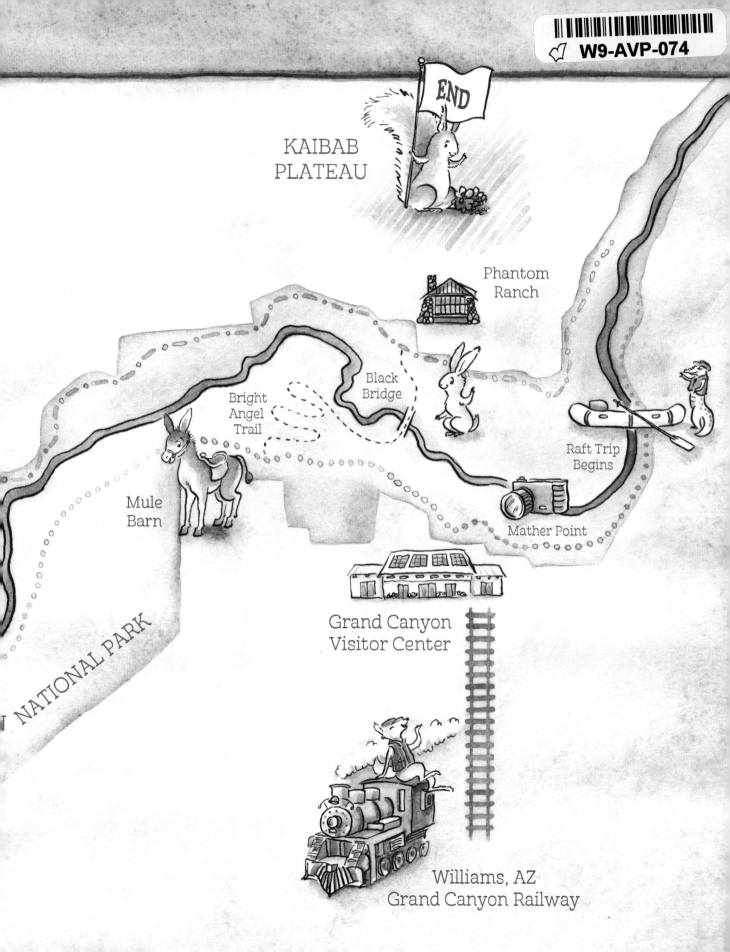

END

KAIBAB
PLATEAU

Phantom
Ranch

Black
Bridge

Bright
Angel
Trail

Raft Trip
Begins

Mule
Barn

Mather Point

Grand Canyon
Visitor Center

NATIONAL PARK

Williams, AZ
Grand Canyon Railway

Tino the Tortoise

Adventures in the Grand Canyon

Written by

Carolyn L. Ahern

Illustrated by

Erik Brooks

WESTWINDS
PRESS®

Library of Congress Cataloging-in-Publication Data

Ahern, Carolyn L.
  Tino the Tortoise : adventures in the Grand Canyon /
by Carolyn Ahern ; illustrated by Erik Brooks.
    pages cm
  ISBN 978-1-941821-45-9 (hardcover)
  I. Brooks, Erik, 1972- illustrator. II. Title.
  PZ7.A268779Tg 2015
  [E]—dc23

                    2014034699

Editor: Michelle McCann
Designer: Vicki Knapton

Published by WestWinds Press®
An imprint of

GRAPHIC ARTS
BOOKS®

P.O. Box 56118
Portland, Oregon 97238-6118
503-254-5591
www.graphicartsbooks.com

The author has designated a portion of her royalties
from the sale of this book to be donated to the
Grand Canyon Association.

Disclaimer notice: While the author and publisher have
made every effort to provide accurate information in
this book, the author and publisher do not assume and
disclaim any liability to any party for loss or damage
caused by errors or omission. Anyone planning a trip to
the Grand Canyon should always check first with park
service officials and tour operators. The activities in the
park are subject to park rules and operator availability
and will vary by the expedition. Please refer to:
www.nps.gov/grca

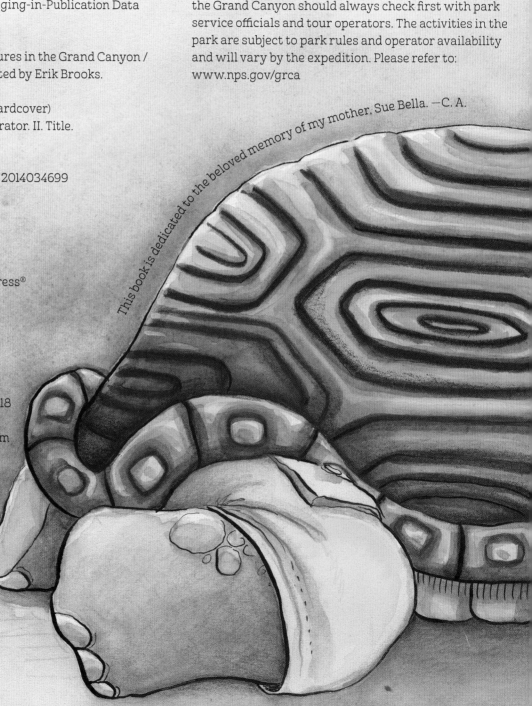

This book is dedicated to the beloved memory of my mother, Sue Bella. —C. A.

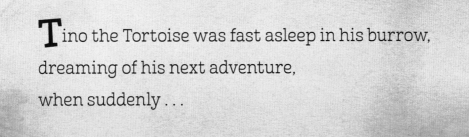

Tino the Tortoise was fast asleep in his burrow,
dreaming of his next adventure,
when suddenly . . .

"Tino! Wake up!" It was his friend Rudi, the long-eared jerboa. "I just read in *Tortoise Talk* that the Kaibab squirrel needs our help."

"Why?" asked a sleepy Tino.

"Penny the Kaibab squirrel wrote that they eat seeds from the cone of the ponderosa pine tree, but they are getting tired of eating the same thing, day after day," said Rudi. "She asked readers to mail in recipes. I have one to share: roasted pine seeds and honey."

"Mmmm, I love those!" said Tino. "How about we take your recipe to Penny in person? It would be an adventure."

"But where do we find her?" asked Rudi.

Tino pulled out a map and found a likely spot:

Arizona's Kaibab National Forest.

"That's right next to the Grand Canyon," said Tino. "Why don't we explore while we're there? I'll call ahead and make reservations."

"Count me in!" said Rudi.

So Rudi wrote down his recipe and they started on their way.

Tino and Rudi walked down the desert trail and soon met up with an owl.

"Where are you going?" the owl asked.

"We are searching for Penny, the Kaibab squirrel," said Tino, showing him the picture from the paper.

"Ah yes . . . the Kaibab squirrel has a fondness for pine seeds, as I recall.
You must go to the end of this trail, and then ride the train until you reach
the big hole in the ground," instructed the owl.

"How big is the hole?" asked Tino.

"Oh, it's big," said the owl. "You can't miss it."

So Tino and Rudi continued on their way.

After a lot of walking they finally reached the train station.

"ALL ABOARD!" called the conductor. Tino and Rudi hopped on.

"Next stop: the Grand Canyon."

Tino and Rudi watched the landscape change from tumbleweeds and sagebrush to green forest and pine trees. But there was no sign of Penny.

As they rode, they listened to the conductor: "The Grand Canyon is one of the Natural Wonders of the World. The canyon is, on average, one mile deep, 10 miles wide, and is 277 miles long. The Colorado River has been carving the steep canyon walls over millions of years."

SHRIIIEEEEK! the train's brakes squealed.

"End of the line," announced the conductor, "the South Rim of Grand Canyon National Park."

Tino and Rudi caught a shuttle bus to the lookout at Mather Point.

"Wow!" said Rudi.

"So *that's* what the owl meant by a 'big hole in the ground'!" laughed Tino.

They looked around at the Visitor Center, but still no sign of Penny. Rudi asked a park ranger, "We are looking for Kaibab squirrels. Have you seen them?"

"Sure. We call them 'tassel-eared squirrels' because of the long fur on their ears. They also have dark bellies and snowy white tails," the ranger explained. "You'll find them in the ponderosa pine trees."

PLANTS OF THE GRAND CANYON

"What do the trees look like?" asked Tino.

"You can tell a ponderosa by the deep, dark cracks in its bark. And its needles grow in groups of three," she explained. "But your squirrels live only on the Kaibab Plateau, which is on the other side of the canyon."

"How do we get there?" asked Rudi.

"We've got reservations for a mule ride down into the canyon," Tino explained.

"Really?" asked Rudi, who was nervous and excited at the same time.

When they arrived at the mule corral, a wrangler helped them saddle up. They took the Bright Angel Trail, which drops over 4,000 feet from the top of the canyon rim all the way down to the Colorado River at the bottom.

Along the way they saw petroglyphs—rock carvings made by Native Americans of long ago. **"Yikes!** This trail is so high and narrow!" Rudi cried.

"Don't worry. The mules are careful and they're used to zigzagging their way down the switchbacks," said Tino.

Rudi closed his eyes.

A voice called out from the bushes, **"WHOA!"**

As the line of mules jerked to a stop, a rabbit appeared, pointing at the slope. "Hold up, big horn sheep ahead." The group waited as the sheep crossed the trail.

"Whew!" Tino sighed. "Thanks."

"No problem," said the rabbit. "Where ya headed?"

"We are searching for Kaibab squirrels," said Rudi. "We're bringing them a recipe."

"Those fluffy-eared squirrels are easy to spot," said the rabbit. "Just look for the nests they build out of twigs and pine needles. And when they eat pine seeds, they leave a pile of cobs behind. I can show you the way, but why not stop by my place for a cool drink first?"

Tino and Rudi were thirsty. "Sure!" they agreed.

As they crossed over Black Bridge, Tino shouted, "We're at the bottom of the canyon now, but the Colorado River is still so far below us!"

Rudi giggled, "Tino! Your binoculars are backwards!"

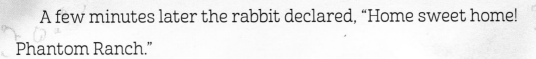

A few minutes later the rabbit declared, "Home sweet home! Phantom Ranch."

They sipped the cool water then looked for shady spots to rest. Out of nowhere, a new voice warned, "I wouldn't sit there if I were you."

Tino was about to sit on a snake! He popped inside his shell and the snake darted away.

"Shoot! There goes lunch," said a roadrunner.

"You eat those?" asked Rudi.

"Yep," he answered.

Tino popped his head out. "This time *I* was almost lunch. Thanks!"

"Where are you headed?" asked the roadrunner.

"We're on our way to Boat Beach," said Tino. "I reserved us two seats on a white-water raft. We're going to float down the Colorado River!"

"We are?" asked Rudi, who was nervous and excited at the same time.

At Boat Beach, their guide was waiting for them. They hopped on their raft and floated the blue-green water of the river. For hours they gazed up at the enormous canyon walls, soaring sandstone cliffs, and colorful layers of rock. As evening approached, they set up camp on one of the river's many beaches.

They had lots of questions. "How long is the Colorado River?" asked Rudi.

"1,450 miles long," said their guide.

"Are there lots of rapids?" asked Tino.

"More than 150, some easy and some hard."

Just then, a huge shadow swooped over them. "Yikes!" yelled Rudi, as a bald eagle dove.

"Don't worry, I've got you covered!" said Tino, guarding him with his sturdy shell.

The next day their relaxing raft ride began to change. . . .

Tino noticed the water swirling faster and faster! "Uh-oh! Watch out ahead!" he shouted.

"Uh . . . Tino? It's getting pretty bumpy. What's happening?" cried Rudi.

"Hold on everyone! We're gonna take a plunge!" hollered their guide.

Down and up, up and down went the raft. Tino and Rudi laughed and screamed with excitement as they bounced down the rapids.

Over the next few days, they rode through thrilling rapids and calm waters. Before long, they arrived at Diamond Creek.

"We made it!" Tino cried. They thanked their guide and headed for the bus.

Once they got back to the Bright Angel Lodge, they caught a rim-to-rim shuttle. As they drove toward the North Rim of the canyon, Rudi and Tino saw a forest of ponderosa pine trees. They were finally nearing Penny's home.

When the bus stopped at the Grand Canyon Lodge, they couldn't believe how green it was compared to the reds and browns of the canyon below.

Deep in the forest, they heard an encouraging noise: **Squeak, squeak, chatter, chatter.**

"We must be close!" said Rudi, feeling nervous and excited at the same time.

Tino showed Rudi a pile of pinecone cobs.

"Look!" cried Rudi, "a squirrel nest!"

A furry head poked out from the branches.
There was no mistaking those tasseled ears!

"Hi, I'm Rudi and this is my friend Tino. We're looking for Penny."

"That's me!" said the squirrel.

"We read your article and brought you our favorite recipe: roasted pine seeds and honey," said Rudi.

"Thank you," said Penny, "I'm so excited to try something new."

"How about if we cook up Rudi's recipe for dinner tonight?" suggested Tino.

"I'm getting hungry just thinking about it," said Penny.

That night they feasted on honey-roasted pine seeds with their new squirrel friends. They listened to the wind blowing through the ponderosa pines and stared up at the river of stars until they couldn't keep their eyes open.

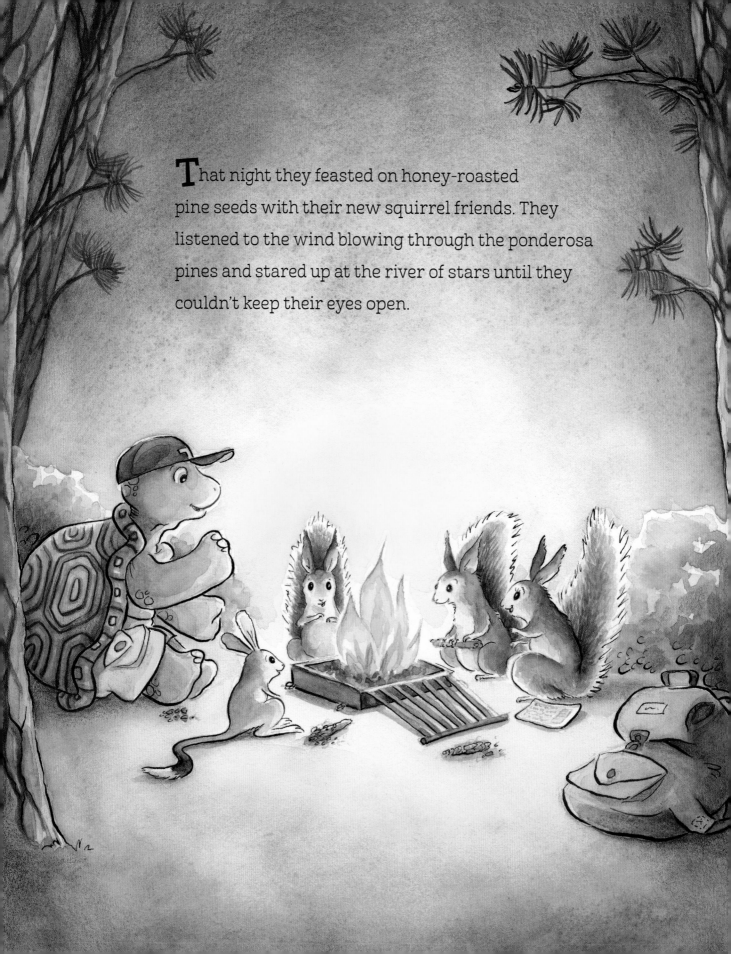

The next morning they said their good-byes.

"Thanks for having us," said Rudi.

"Come visit us in the Mojave Desert sometime," said Tino. "We'll be sure to have a new pine seed recipe for you."

"I promise," said Penny.

Mission accomplished, Tino and Rudi headed for home.

"I love the Grand Canyon and the Kaibab National Forest, but I'm ready to be back in our burrow," said Rudi.

"Me, too," said Tino.

Author's Note

The Grand Canyon is known for its majestic views, which reveal billions of years of geological history. The brilliantly colored North and South Rims rise up from the Colorado River, creating a huge canyon filled with a unique diversity of plants and animals, including the fascinating Kaibab squirrel (*Sciurus kaibabensis*).

You can tell this charismatic critter by its tufted ears, fluffy white tail, brown back, and black or sometimes gray belly. The only place in the world where you will find this squirrel is the Kaibab Plateau, which consists of the North Rim of Grand Canyon National Park and the Kaibab National Forest. There the Kaibab squirrel and the ponderosa pine depend on each other. The squirrels eat the pine seeds, inner bark, twigs, buds, and the pollen cones, and they nest and raise their young in the tree's branches. During the harsh winters, the squirrels get nutrients from a fungus that grows around the tree's roots. This fungus allows the tree to absorb more water and minerals. The Kaibab squirrels help the ponderosa by spreading the fungi spores to trees all around the forest. Because of this symbiotic relationship, both squirrel and tree flourish and remain healthy.

The delicately balanced ecosystem of the North Rim of Grand Canyon National Park and the Kaibab National Forest is maintained under the watchful eyes and dedication of the National Park Service, U.S. Forest Service, conservation organizations, and volunteers. I hope that Tino and his friend Rudi inspire you to visit the Grand Canyon and Kaibab National Forest, to appreciate their unique beauty, and to be good stewards of your national parks for future generations.

Tino the Tortoise
Adventures in the Grand Canyon